MAMBA

ANGELA DUNGEE-FARLEY

ISBN: 1461032164
ISBN-13: 9781461032168

DEDICATION

To my boys, son Daniel and husband Dennis.
Thank you for your support during this wonderful
endeavor...........especially you Daniel,
mommies little motivator.

TABLE OF CONTENTS

The black in "black mamba' does not refer to the color of this deadly snake's body, but rather to the highly pigmented lining of its mouth. Native to the savannas and rocky hills of Southern and Eastern Africa, the black mamba is considered the longest, fastest, and most deadly of the venomous snakes on land. The average black mamba can reach a maximum length of fourteen feet and achieve speeds tracked at ten to twelve miles per hour. It is able to lift about two-thirds of its body off the ground and strike from a distance of four to six feet away. Without treatment, its potent venom can be 100 percent fatal in less than fifteen minutes of being bitten. With this being the case, why would anyone even consider amplifying these attributes?

Well, man's never-ending quest to make what's perfect better is the bane of his existence and will inevitably be the cause of his demise.

CAST OF CHARACTERS

Black Mamba	genetically engineered snake
George Fields	tech (underachiever, low self-esteem, cowardly)
Dr. Neal Stanford	researcher who's specialty is genetic engineering (obnoxious, vain, arrogant, genius, borderline psychotic)
Dr. Helena Merit	assistant to Dr. Stanford (driven, motivated, admires Dr. Stanford's genius)
Mr. Grant	ruthless criminal
Three Henchmen	men who work for Mr. Grant
Mr. Haywood	worksite supervisor
Jackie-O	warehouse worker (fun-loving, full of antics, wants to be cool)
Jackson (Jax) Lang	warehouse worker (leader, heroic type, has a secret)

Lacy Haverton	warehouse worker (smart, beautiful, team player)
Joanne Lafferty	secretary (neurotic, nervous, anal, timid)
Carlos Dejesus	warehouse worker (brute, rough around the edges, bully type, dependable)
Claude Cooper	warehouse worker (not a team player, conceited, self-absorbed)
Linwood Cassidy	warehouse worker (all-around nice guy)
Spencer Mason	warehouse worker (substance abuser, irresponsible, careless)
Vagrant	homeless man living outside of the facility

SETTING / BACKGROUND

In an underground facility, a small group of scientists, who were supposed to be studying the mating habits of the black mamba and the effects of its venom while in captivity, were actually conducting genetic experiments—seeking to find ways to increase the mambas' length, speed, agility, intelligence, and, most important, its aggression. The lead scientist, Dr. Neal Stanford, was fascinated with the natural attributes the black mamba possessed and had spent a lifetime trying to alter them. He was obsessed with creating a new species of mamba, one "God" did not have a hand in creating. His vanity or borderline insanity left no room for remorse or reason. His goal was to create an animal that would truly be an adversary of man—keen, clever, and of course controlled only by him.

SCENE 1:
AT THE
UNDERGROUND FACILITY

Background: A male and female black mamba mate while in captivity, successfully producing five genetically enhanced/engineered eggs. Luckily for George the tech, he was on-site that night at the time of the deliveries, so he sneaks into the lab and steals one of the egg as payment on a debt he owes a local loan shark. He reports only four eggs to Dr. Stanford.

GEORGE

Hey, little guys, you're finally here. I don't know what all the hoopla is about, but you must be something special for this group of nerds to be keeping you top secret. Well, there are five of you, so I don't think they'll mind if I help myself to one.

Using a gripper to hold down the head of the weakened mother, George steals one of the eggs. He's planning to negotiate a deal with a local criminal and report only four eggs to his boss. The mother mamba begins to try to get away from the grip.

GEORGE

Hold on, little mamma. I just need one of these little guys in order to get out of some trouble. I promise you nothing bad will happen to him. Who would have ever thought that an egg would be my salvation? I hope Mr. Grant has faith in you as well.

George hears movement outside the door of the lab.

GEORGE

I'd better get outta here; the last thing I'd want is to be caught carrying you out.

SCENE 2:
BACK IN THE FACILITY
THE NEXT MORNING

The following morning, George is already in the lab when Dr. Stanford enters. George rushes over to welcome him.

GEORGE

Good morning, sir. They're here!

He gestures toward the pile of genetically enhanced eggs.

Dr. Stanford walks across the room toward the cage holding the eggs.

DR. STANFORD

How many are there?

GEORGE

Four, sir. Aren't they great?

DR. STANFORD

Has Dr. Merit been made aware?

Dr. Merit enters the room. Dr. Helena Merit whose sole purpose is to serve Dr. Stanford her mentor, her hero.

DR. MERIT

I'm here.

She walks over to the cage and looks in amazement at the eggs.

DR. MERIT

Absolutely magnificent!

George is eager to impress.

GEORGE

Dr. Stanford would you like for me to—

Dr. Stanford sharply cuts George short.

DR. STANFORD

That will be all, George.

George timidly begins to walk away but is immediately summoned back by Dr. Stanford.

DR. STANFORD

Oh, by the way George…

George stops and looks back, enthused.

GEORGE

Yes, sir?

DR. STANFORD

Get down to the subbasement and clean out those cages. It's absolutely filthy down there. Keeping that area clean is one of your responsibilities. Don't make me have to remind you again.

George walks away timidly, speaking as he goes.

GEORGE

Yes, sir.

Dr. Stanford turns his attention to Dr. Merit.

> DR. STANFORD
>
> Yes, magnificent indeed. With the accelerated hormones coursing through them, these masters will far exceed their ancestors. With speeds reaching anywhere from twenty to thirty miles per hour, lengths reaching at least twenty feet, amazing agility, and most importantly an intelligence and aggression never before seen, this generation of mambas will be faster, smarter, and of course deadlier. These magnificent creatures that were once hunted by man will be the hunters of man.

Dr. Merit has a devious smile on her face.

> DR. MERIT
>
> Pure death.

Dr. Stanford is confident of his success.

DR. STANFORD

Finally, my vision will be recognized and envied by those in the world of genetic research who once ostracized and ridiculed me. They will kneel before me with admiration and regret the day they ever defied my genius.

SCENE 3:
OUTSIDE THE FACILITY IN AN ALLEYWAY

George has sneaked out of the facility to meet Mr. Grant, the ruthless loan shark he's indebted to. They meet in a nearby alleyway to negotiate a deal for the debt George owes him. Mr. Grant is surrounded by his henchmen.

MR. GRANT

George, do you have my money?

George is obviously nervous. He is fidgeting, stuttering, his eyes darting around.

GEORGE

Hi, Mr. Grant. I have something
for you much more valuable than
money.

MR. GRANT

My money, George, all I want is my
money.

George stands there holding a box; inside is the egg he's
stolen.

GEORGE

But I have something in this box far
more valuable than the money I owe
you. Here, take a look.

George opens the box. Mr. Grant is amused at first and
makes a joke of it.

MR. GRANT

An egg, George? A freaking egg!
What am I supposed to do with this?
Fry it?

Mr. Grant's henchmen start to laugh.

Mr. Grants shifts back into a serious mood.

MR. GRANT

Are you playing games with me, George? You know I'm a man of business.

GEORGE

No, Mr. Grant, I'm not playing games. I know this egg is something special. I could tell just by the way those doctors were talking about it.

Mr. Grant is not pleased with George's response.

MR. GRANT

I'm just supposed to believe this egg is worth something because you say so, George? Are you trying to make a fool out of me?

George starts to feel a little uncomfortable, a little leery.

GEORGE

No, Mr. Grant. I heard those doctors talking, and I know they would be willing to pay a pretty penny to get this egg back. I got it from the lab where I work. They're always doing things behind closed doors—secret stuff.

Mr. Grant is not impressed with George's reasoning and has no choice but to make an example of him.

MR. GRANT

I'm going to have to teach you a lesson and send a message to my other customers who think they can get money from me and not pay it back.

George is becoming more frightened.

GEORGE

Please, Mr. Grant, this egg could make you a rich man. Those doctors have been doing some top-secret work with those snakes and their eggs. That's how I know this little one is something special.

MR. GRANT

Save it, George. I'm already a rich man. No thanks to losers like you.

Mr. Grants pulls out a gun and points it at George. George pleads with him not to pull the trigger.

GEORGE

No, Mr. Grant, please.

But his plea is futile.

GEORGE

No, Mr. Grant, please.

Mr. Grant shoots George and simply stands there watching as George drops to his knees. Poor George kneels holding his stomach, blood pouring out over his hands. He looks down at the blood dripping down over his hands onto the ground. His eyes begin to weaken, and he falls to the ground. As this is unfolding, he drops the box onto the ground. The egg rolls out of the box and down through a grid in the street.

SCENE 4:
UNDER THE STREET

Time passes, approximately three months, and the egg begins to bulge. Something is pushing it from the inside.

SCENE 5:
AT THE FACILITY,
SEVERAL WEEKS LATER

The egg has now hatched, and the snake has matured—actually, it has grown beyond the length of a natural mamba. It has made its way through a tunnel, which leads directly back into the underground research facility previously occupied by the scientists responsible for its existence. Why did it go back? Perhaps it is the close proximity of where it hatched to the location of the lab or just a sense that this is home. The facility has been abandoned by the former occupants and is now being used by a group of warehouse workers unaware of the previous activity and of the danger that lurks within.

It is 2:45p.m. and the evening shift is about to get started. The workers who are now occupying the warehouse are in the upper-level conference room congregating when Mr. Haywood, the worksite supervisor, walks in.

> MR. HAYWOOD
>
> Hey, listen up. I have overtime for anyone willing to stick around tonight.

Jackie-O, a self-proclaimed "Mr. Cool," turns to Jax Lang, a mysterious type who has recently joined the crew.

> JACKIE-O
>
> That's a double shift. Hey, my man, if you're up to it, I am.
>
> JAX
>
> Don't you have a hot date or something tonight?

Jackie-O looks confused by Jax's comment.

> JACKIE-O
>
> Hey, where you hear that?

With a grin on his face, Jax picks up his property and puts it in his bag.

JAX

Well, the hot phone call you were
having earlier today, and those.

Jax looks in the opposite direction, but Jackie-O still
doesn't get it.

JACKIE-O

What?

Jax nods his head toward Jackie-O's duffle bag, indicating
the pack of condoms sticking out.

JACKIE-O

Oh man, good catch. I knew you
were cool from the first time we
met. Hey, anything going on with
you...

Jackie-O punches Jax on the arm and nods his head toward
one of the warehouse workers—the young, sexy, and outspoken Lacy Haverton.

JACKIE-O

And that?

Lacy being outspoken and direct as usual responds to
Mr. Haywood's request.

LACY

I'll stick around; I can always use the
extra money.

MR. HAYWOOD

Now, I can't promise you'll see that
money on your next paycheck, but
believe me, it's coming.

Lacy responds sarcastically.

LACY

Great, the story of my life, broken
promises.

Jackie-O interrogates Jax in his self-confident manner.

JACKIE-O

Hey, is anything going on there? If so,
I'll just back up, give you a chance.
You know, I'll do that for a friend.

Jax smiles.

JAX

Look, I'm just here for the work; no
intention of planting roots, so don't
mind me.

JACKIE-O

Not planting roots? You sound like a
man with a past.

He leans over close to Jax and speaks in a suspicious tone.

JACKIE-O

Or should I say a secret past?

JAX

No, just don't want anything holding me back from moving on. I guess
I'm what you would call a "drifter."

Jackie-O leans back in again and speaks in a low and self-
assured tone.

JACKIE-O

Well, just giving you a head start,
my man, because once I move in on
her, no average Joe stands a chance.

Jax strokes Jackie-O's ego.

JAX

I hear you lover boy. Go for it.

Joanne Lafferty, the neurotic and socially impaired secretary, is sitting across the room at her desk.

>JOANNE
>
>Well, I'll stay for a little while, but it's not a good idea for a woman to be down here too late at night.

There's a note of disgust in her voice.

>JOANNE
>
>I can only imagine what elements come out down here once the sun goes down and what they're up to.

Jackie-O leans over to Jax and whispers.

>JACKIE-O
>
>I bet you one thing: whatever they're up to, she's not on the itinerary.

Then he laughs under his breath.

The loud and self-assured "muscleman," Carlos DeJesus, sits at the edge of the conference room table twirling his pride and joy, a knife—but not just any knife, a big-ass hunting knife. He yells out to the others.

CARLOS

I'll stick around, but I have to give
my old lady a call to let her know
I'll be in much later tonight. She
gets crazy when I come in late. Hell,
she's gone as far as locking and bolt-
ing the door, so you know I go off,
and before I know it, I'm kicking
the damn door in.

He starts pumping his biceps.

CARLOS

I don't realize my own strength
sometimes. Then those freaking
neighbors get involved, and before
you know it, the cops show up.

Carlos's monologue is interrupted by the very rude and
obnoxious Claude Cooper, who speaks in a sarcastic tone.

CLAUDE

And we all know how important
your brute strength is to you.

Carlos responds to Claude's comment in an accusatory
tone.

CARLOS

Yes, and what's wrong with that?
Every man should take pride in
his physique, his stature, hell, his
manhood.

Claude replies condescendingly.

CLAUDE

I hear you, big guy.

He pats Carlos's shoulder as he passes by.

Another one of the warehouse workers, Linwood Cassidy,
enters the room.

LINWOOD

Hey, guys. where's Mason?

Spencer Mason is a co-worker with a substance-abuse
problem, who spends most of his time sleeping or getting
high in the locker room. Jackie-O speaks under his breath
to Jax.

JACKIE-O

Probably somewhere getting a "high
five."

SCENE 6:
IN THE LOCKER ROOM

Mason, as he is commonly called by his co-workers, is in the locker room, nodding off. He is so high he can barely stand when Mr. Haywood calls him over the intercom.

MR. HAYWOOD

Hey, Spencer, will you be able to work late tonight?

Mr. Haywood does not get a response.

MR. HAYWOOD

Hey, Mason, where are you? Or should I say, what are you up to?

Spencer staggers to his feet in order to talk into the intercom; he's barely able to hold on to the phone and speak at the same time.

SPENCER

Hey, yes, I'm here.

MR. HAYWOOD

I know you're here. What I want to know is will you be able to stay late tonight? Do a little overtime?

Spencer tries to pull himself together. He is barely able to.

SPENCER

Yeah, I'll stay.

MR. HAYWOOD

Well, get your butt up here. I'm not paying you overtime to just sit around.

There's silence.

MR. HAYWOOD

Hey, Spencer!

SPENCER

Yes?

MR. HAYWOOD

Make sure you have your head on straight tonight; my workers' comp hasn't kicked in yet.

Both men hang up the intercoms.

SCENE 7:
IN THE WAREHOUSE

It is 3:00p.m. and Mr. Haywood collects his belongings as he's about to leave.

MR. HAYWOOD

Well, I'm out of here. See you guys in the morning.

Linwood throws in his comical "two cents."

LINWOOD

Hey, how do you get to get out of here on time?

MR. HAYWOOD

I'm the boss.

Linwood smiles.

LINWOOD

You'll get no argument here.

JOANNE

Mr. Haywood, don't forget…

She blows her nose.

JOANNE

We need to go over the inventory
tomorrow to make sure everything
is accounted for.

She continues with an attitude.

JOANNE

You know how things just seem
to…walk away around here.

Mr. Haywood responds with an agreeable tone.

MR. HAYWOOD

Yes, Joanne, remind me when I get
in tomorrow.

JOANNE

Yes, sir.

Mr. Haywood picks up his belongings to leave for the day.

MR. HAYWOOD

Okay, see you all tomorrow.

He turns and looks back.

MR. HAYWOOD

And by the way, get some work
done.

Linwood reassures Mr. Haywood.

LINWOOD

Will do, boss.

JACKIE-O

Hey, speak for yourself.

SCENE 8:
IN ANOTHER PART OF
THE WAREHOUSE

Mr. Haywood is making his way down the corridor leading to the exit door unaware of the danger awaiting him. He is humming a tune and looking forward to the remainder of his evening.

SCENE 9:
IN THE WAREHOUSE
CONFERENCE ROOM

Back in the conference room, Jax makes his way over to where Lacy is sitting.

> JAX
>
> Well, with all the stock he has in the back, I think it's safe to say this is going to be an all-nighter.

She looks at him and replies flirtatiously.

> LACY
>
> You have a problem with that? Perhaps you had some other plans for the night?

JAX

No, just an observation.

LACY

I see...Well, since we've not been officially introduced, my name is Lacy Haverton.

He reaches out to shake her hand.

JAX

Hi, Jax Lang.

Lacy is curious.

LACY

You're new around here, aren't you?

He hesitates.

JAX

Yes, just passing through. What about yourself?

She nods her head.

LACY

I've been here a few years, not much opportunity in this town for someone with just a GED. I've seen you around, but you're usually coming in and I'm usually finishing up my shift and on the way out.

JAX

Yes, that's the disadvantage of having employees working different shifts; you never really get a chance to meet all your co-workers.

LACY

Some may say that's actually a big advantage.

Jax stands there looking on as she walks away.

Jackie-O walks over to Jax and speaks in a condescending tone.

JACKIE-O

Whatever happened to, I'm just here to work, not planting roots?

Jax responds with a smile on his face.

JAX

And I stand by that.

JACKIE-O

Well, you'd better. I'll be keeping an eye on you.

Jax just smiles and walks away.

Jackie-O mutters to himself.

JACKIE-O

The nerve of him trying to be a "player."

SCENE 10:
THE EXIT DOOR

Back at the exit door, Mr. Haywood, still humming and in good spirits, is about to punch in the code when he thinks he hears something. He turns and looks around.

MR. HAYWOOD

Hey, is somebody there?

Mamba looks on, watching, lurking, stalking just beyond the lights, anticipating its attack as a predator anticipates its prey. Mr. Haywood proceeds with punching in his code.

MR. HAYWOOD

Come on, come on! What's the matter with this damn thing? I've only punched in this code hundreds of times.

He is still trying to punch in the correct code.

MR. HAYWOOD

Damn numbers are so small.

He hears the noise again.

MR. HAYWOOD

Who's there? This isn't funny, guys.

This time, he's a little unsettled and decides to take a look around.

SCENE 11:
THE CONFERENCE ROOM

While Mr. Haywood tries to find the source of the noise, back in the conference room, the team is about to get to work on the stock.

> LINWOOD
>
> I'm going to get started on that new inventory out back.

As he's about to walk away, he turns back.

> LINWOOD
>
> Anyone care to join me?

Jackie-O hesitates and then steps up.

JACKIE-O

Hell, I'll help. It's going to be a long night. I'll do anything to make it go by faster.

Linwood's fine with that.

LINWOOD

Let's do it.

SCENE 12:
NEAR THE EXIT DOOR

At the opposite end of the building, Mr. Haywood is again attempting to punch in the correct code in order to exit the building.

> MR. HAYWOOD
>
>> Hell, let me take out these "distance"—as they call them—reading glasses and get out of here.

With his left hand, he reaches into the right chest pocket of his jacket and retrieves his eyeglasses. He holds them out in front of him and looks through them while punching in the code.

MR. HAYWOOD

I think I have it this time.

He suddenly stops, sensing that he's not alone. Being true to its nature, mamba slithers up behind Mr. Haywood. He stands still, *very* still, aware that someone or—worse—something is behind him. Mr. Haywood continues to stand at attention, one hand on the keypad, the other still holding his eyeglasses at a distance. Mr. Haywood can hear what sounds like a heavy hissing, and then he feels something crawl up his leg, over his thigh, and up and around his torso, proceeding to just behind his right shoulder, but he's too afraid to make a move. Now through the reflection of his eyeglasses, he's able to see with disbelief what has descended upon him.

Mr. Haywood now has a reflection of himself in the left eyeglass lens and in the right lens a reflection of Mamba. He has now come face-to-face with his assassin. Mr. Haywood drops his eyeglasses, and as any terrified human would do, he panics and reacts, reaching to pull Mamba away, but his attempt is futile. He's not fast enough, and Mamba wraps its head around and sticks its fangs into Mr. Haywood's throat. And the struggle begins. Blood drains down Mr. Haywood's chest, and as the two struggle, Mr. Haywood's head slams into the keypad, destroying it and making it impossible for the door to open now. The two continue to struggle, and the electrical box is destroyed, causing the lights to temporarily go off; this also affects the lights in the conference room leaving everyone wondering why the lights went out, and then the backup generator kicks in.

As the battle continues, Mr. Haywood struggles to pull Mamba off and to break the snake's grip on his throat, but Mr. Haywood is no match for Mamba, who's determined to bring its victim down. Eventually, a defeated Mr. Haywood loses momentum, staggers, and slowly drops to the floor behind a stack of boxes with Mamba's fangs deadlocked in his throat. Once Mamba's lifeless victim drops to the floor, it releases its grip and victoriously slithers away. This new breed of Mamba is a true adversary to man. It does not hunt man as a natural instinct of survival but as a warrior. The days of humbly slithering away as man approaches to avoid a confrontation is obviously a thing of the past.

SCENE 13:
THE CONFERENCE ROOM

Back in the conference room, the others, unaware of Mr. Haywood's demise, scramble about trying to assess the fallout of the electrical outage. Lacy turns to Jax.

> LACY
>
> What do you think happened?
>
> JAX
>
> I don't know, but that backup generator is only going to cover a few things and the computer is not one.

Carlos sounds annoyed.

CARLOS

Haywood, with his thrifty self, figures he would go cheap on the generators.

LACY

At least we have lights.

Carlos tries to use his cell phone. He speaks in an angry tone.

CARLOS

Hell, I forgot we're too far down for the cell phones to work.

Joanne is frantically checking the telephones.

JOANNE

The house phones seem to be out, too.

She speaks in an uneasy tone.

JOANNE

This can't be good. I knew I shouldn't have stayed late tonight.

Jax tries to get a handle on everything.

JAX

Everyone calm down; we should be
all right. At least with the generator,
we have lights, and since we're only
loading stock, we should be able to
make it through the night.

CLAUDE

And who put you in charge?

Jax replies in a patient tone.

JAX

Look, I'm not in charge. I'm just
trying to make it through the night.

Linwood and Jackie-O return to the conference room.

LINWOOD

Anyone know what happened?

JAX

No, your guess is as good as mine.

Linwood reiterates what Jax has already stated.

LINWOOD

Well, we only have to be down here till morning, so it should be okay. Look, if we all work together on loading the inventory, we may be able to get out of here earlier. Okay?

Jackie-O takes the lead.

JACKIE-O

Sounds good to me.

LINWOOD

So let's get to it.

As Linwood is about to walk away, he stops.

LINWOOD

Hey, has anyone seen Mason?

He waits for a response, but there is none.

LINWOOD

Anyone willing to make a guess as to where he could be?

Carlos states the obvious.

CARLOS

The better question would be what's
he up to?

At first, Jax hesitates.

JAX

I'll go down to the locker room;
he's probably there.

LACY

I'll go with you, Jax. You will probably need a little help with getting
him on his feet. Besides he can be a
tirade at times.

As Jax and Lacy begin to walk away, Joanne speaks in a
nervous tone.

JOANNE

Wait, I don't want to stay here by
myself. I'm going with you guys.

Jax addresses the rest of the team.

JAX

After we get Mason, we'll meet you
guys in the stockroom.

SCENE 14:
ON THE WAY TO
THE LOCKER ROOM

Everyone has disbursed to their designated areas. Jax, Lacy, and Joanne go looking for Mason; all the others go to the stockroom.

> LACY
>
> I can't wait to get finished and get
> out of here.

Jax smiles.

> JAX
>
> Now that sounds like someone with
> plans for the night.

LACY

No, it's just been a long week, and
since Haywood doesn't seem to
know exactly when the overtime
will be—well, I'm just not in the
mood to do charity work. But since
I said I'd stay, I'm on board.

Joanne responds in her usual neurotic and timid tone.

JOANNE

Well, I'm starting to get a bad
feeling.

Lacy is beginning to feel concerned.

LACY

A bad feeling? A bad feeling about
what, Joanne?

JOANNE

I don't know, but I'm starting
to feel I should have left when
Mr. Haywood left.

Jax was the voice of reason.

JAX

Okay, let's get Mason, get the job done, and get out of here. How does that sound?

Lacy nods in agreement.

LACY

Sounds good to me.

They proceed in the direction of the locker room.

SCENE 15:
IN THE LOCKER ROOM

In the locker room, Mason is now either very intoxicated or high or both. In any event, he has decided to crash on the cot. As an incapacitated Spencer Mason attempts to sleep off his high, notorious Mamba slithers into the room with every intention of making Mason its next conquest. As Spencer Mason lies asleep in a drunken stupor, snoring, Mamba makes its way underneath the blanket covering him. Mamba's outline is visible as it winds itself underneath the blanket from the foot toward the head of the cot. Mamba continues to ascend toward Mason but stops suddenly whenever Mason moves, careful not to wake its prey. Then Mamba strikes, and with both hands, Mason grabs the blanket covering him with a grip so tight it would have strangled an ox. Both eyes pop wide open as if electronically, but there is no life behind them. Mason begins sweating profusely and salivating from the mouth. As he's nearing his end, he loses control of his mouth and tongue, but just before the end, he suffers severe shortness of breath and violent convulsions, and then he dies. There lies Mason's remains, his face black and blue, his purple tongue profusely swollen and sticking out of his mouth.

SCENE 16:
THE LOADING AREA

Down in the loading area working on inventory, Jackie-O is talking to Linwood in a tone of mock envy.

> JACKIE-O
>
> Hell, we're down here working our butts off, and my man Jax is up there with the girl, or girls if you include Lady Joanne.

He then laughs.

Linwood smiles and gives him support.

LINWOOD

Better luck next time the lights go
out.

JACKIE-O

You know, you're a funny guy.

Linwood smiles and continues to work.

SCENE 17:
ON THE WAY TO
THE LOCKER ROOM

As Jax, Lacy, and Joanne approach the locker room, Joanne crosses her arms as if to secure herself while looking around.

JOANNE

It's creepy around here at night. I'm only ever here during the daytime, but when Mr. Haywood asked me to stick around to catch up on some paperwork and he offered overtime, I thought it was a good idea.

Joanne was looking unsettled.

JOANNE

But I'm not sure anymore.

LACY

Yes, the old overtime trick. Well, if Haywood's nothing else, he's consistent.

Jax knocks on the door.

JAX

Hey, Mason, time to hit the rocks.

There's silence.

LACY

Knock again. Maybe he didn't hear you.

So Jax knocks again.

JAX

Hey, Mason, we don't have all night. Well, we did before the lights went out. The rest of us want to get the inventory loaded so the trunks can roll on time tomorrow. Are you coming?

There's still silence. Lacy is now looking concerned.

LACY

Maybe something's wrong.

Jax pushes the door open. Mason's lying on the cot dead. Joanne screams.

JOANNE

I'm getting the hell out of here!

She runs out of the room. Lacy tries to stop Joanne from leaving the room but to no avail. She turns her attention back to Mason lying on the cot.

LACY

Jax, what happened to him?

Jax kneels down and checks Mason for signs of life, but there are none.

LACY

Jax, did he overdose?

Jax answers in an ambiguous tone.

JAX

Looks that way.

A frantic Joanne alerts the others, and everyone rushes to the locker room.

>JACKIE-O
>
>Damn, looks like old Mason took his last hit.

Jax responds with uncertainty.

>JAX
>
>Yes, looks that way.

Jackie-O is suspicious of Jax's response.

>JACKIE-O
>
>Why do you say it like that? You think something else happened?

Claude speaks in a patronizing tone.

>CLAUDE
>
>Yes, Jax, do you think something else happened, like maybe one of us made something else happen?
>
>JAX
>
>No, I'm not saying anything like that. It's just that I've seen…

He hesitates.

>JAX

>Never mind.

Lacy moves closer to Jax.

>LACY

>What is it, Jax?

>JAX

>It's just that I've seen one or two OD victims before, and there's something different about this one.

Claude speaks as he's walking away.

>CLAUDE

>Great, we have our very own Sherlock Holmes.

Jax is feeling the weight.

>JAX

>Look, I'm just trying to make sense of what's happened here tonight.

JACKIE-O

Can't it just be a simple overdose? We all know he was on the stuff hard. The only reason Haywood kept him around was because he and Mason's old man were buddies back in the day and because Mason was on parole and needed a job.

Jax hesitates.

JAX

Yes, I guess you're right.

Lacy speaks in a concerned tone.

LACY

What is it, Jax?

JAX

Nothing, it's just that it's been a crazy night.

Linwood intervenes.

LINWOOD

Well, we need to call emergency services.

Jax gets up and walks away. Lacy stares at him as he's walking away, not 100 percent convinced that he's not withholding something. Linwood is holding the telephone.

LINWOOD

Well, the phones are still out, and the cell phone reception down here is hell.

CARLOS

Maybe if we walk around, we can find a location with some reception for the cells. We'll meet you back in the conference room.

Carlos and Linwood walk off together in an attempt to find a location that would provide reception for the cell phones.

SCENE 18:
THE LOCKER ROOM

Lacy pulls Jax to the side.

> LACY
>
> Hey what's going on?

Jax is silent.

> LACY
>
> Look, you may be able to give those guys a song and a dance and they'll accept it, but me, no way, no how.

Jax is still silent.

LACY

Look, if you know something the rest of us should be aware of, or if you even think you know something the rest of us need to be aware of, just spill it, because I have to tell you, I'm starting to feel a little uneasy.

Jax pulls Lacy in closer to him.

JAX

Look, I don't know anything; it's just a feeling I have that something isn't quite right.

She waits for a response with intense curiosity.

LACY

What?

JAX

Okay, as I said, I've seen a couple of ODs, and there's something different about this one.

LACY

Yes?

She's waiting for Jax to continue.

> LACY
>
> What?
>
> JAX
>
> Well, did you happen to notice how twisted his tongue and mouth were?
>
> LACY
>
> Yes.

She pauses and waits for him to continue. When he does not, she prompts him.

> LACY
>
> That's it?
>
> JAX
>
> No, look, I'm no doctor, but neither of the other ODs I've seen had their tongues swollen and sticking out their mouths. His skin was so blue, especially his lips, and his tongue was swollen and bulging out; it looks as if he suffocated.

LACY

Jax that's not a lot to go by, but if he didn't die from an overdose, what do you think happened to him?

JAX

I don't know—a seizure perhaps, heart attack, poison, who knows?

She blurts the word out loudly.

LACY

Poison!

He whispers to her.

JAX

Keep it down. I'm just thinking out loud.

Lacy is becoming fearful.

LACY

You're starting to scare me, but whatever the cause, we need to get the authorities down here.

Jax, Lacy, Jackie-O, Claude, and Joanne go back to the conference room and wait for Carlos and Linwood to return.

SCENE 19:
THE CONFERENCE ROOM

Carlos returns to the conference room.

> CARLOS
>
> Man, no luck out there; this entire place is a dead zone.

Lacy makes a recommendation.

> LACY
>
> Somebody will have to go for help.

Joanne replies nervously.

JOANNE

I just want to get out of here. I just want to go home.

Lacy tries to comfort Joanne.

LACY

No, Joanne, we can't leave; we all need to be here when the authorities come. I'm sure they will want to question all of us when they get here.

Carlos's voice takes on a cautious tone.

CARLOS

What's there to say? We just found him that way.

JACKIE-O

You know the police; every scene is a crime scene even if no crime has been committed.

Jax volunteers.

JAX

I'll go for help.

Claude is being irritating as usual.

> CLAUDE
>
> Here we go. Our hero strikes again.

Lacy tries to derail a confrontation.

> LACY
>
> Come on, Claude, give him a break;
> he's just trying to help here.

Claude leers disgustingly.

> CLAUDE
>
> Lacy, I see you've found your latest
> venture.

Jax approaches Claude to defend Lacy's honor, but she pulls him back.

> JAX
>
> I guess this is your lucky day, Cooper.

> CLAUDE
>
> Is it?

He says this while looking at Lacy with lust on his mind, licking his lips.

CLAUDE

Or is it your lucky day…Jax?

Jax can't take Claude's condescending comments anymore, so he goes for him again, but this time, the two men collide. Jax and Claude start to tangle, pulling and grabbing at each other while exchanging harsh, uncomplimentary words. Lacy and Jackie-O try pulling Jax away while Carlos tries to pull Claude away. Joanne, who is nervous and timid by nature, makes her way to her desk across the room to ensure her safety during the brawl. Lacy is trying to pull Jax away from Claude.

LACY

Hey, guys, this is getting us nowhere.
Jax, he's not worth it.

Claude responds nastily.

CLAUDE

And you are?

JAX

This guy needs his mouth shut—tight.

CLAUDE

And I guess you think you're the one to do it.

Lacy continues trying to pull the two apart.

LACY

Come on, we need to get the authorities down here.

The attempt by Lacy, Jackie-O, and Carlos at breaking the two up is futile, and the conflict continues. They are pulling, grabbing, and taunting each other, hurling verbal insults and threats, too enthralled in their own conflict to notice what is approaching them. Lacy thinks she hears something.

LACY

Wait, guys, did you hear that?

But Jax and Claude continue to struggle. Finally, she's able to get everyone's attention.

LACY

Hey, you hear that?

At this point, the sound is loud enough and close enough to catch everyone's attention—a heavy hissing noise.

The battle between Jax and Claude has stopped, but the two, along with Lacy, Jackie-O, and Carlos, are still clenching one another. All five stand silent, looking in the direction of the hissing sound. Everyone stands huddled together in a fixed position still able to hear the hissing as it gets closer and closer, but they are not yet able to see what it is. Then a silhouette appears on the wall, but what is it? Spotting the shadow on the wall, the five still clench together. They all stare knowing what they see is definitely not good, hoping that the size of the image on the wall is simply exaggerated, enhanced as shadows often are. So they wait, because they know eventually the source of the shadow on the wall will reveal itself. And it does, all magnificent twenty feet of pure superiority, moving in as if a majesty to its throne, gliding effortlessly in as if on air. The five are still huddled together in a fixed position, and Joanne is still over near her desk. Finally, there is a full view of the source of the mysterious hissing, and what a vision—twenty or more linear feet of the most amazing gradient shades of light gray to dark gray scales that seem to go on forever and cold, round, merciless eyes with piercing black pupils, all accompanied by a hissing that weakens their stomachs with fear. Jax is thinking out loud.

JAX

This can't be.

Mamba raises its head and front up off the floor and gives a loud hiss.

JAX

Run!

Everyone disburses in different directions; Lacy and Joanne rush underneath Joanne's desk, while Jax uses a chair to try to ward off the snake. Jackie-O attempts to help Jax but is knocked down and cornered by Mamba. The two are eye to eye.

JACKIE-O

Help! Somebody, help!

Carlos pulls out his knife.

CARLOS

Come on, bitch, and get a piece of this.

Carlos attempts to drive the knife into Mamba, but the snake is too fast and is able to evade his every attempt. In the midst of all the conflict, Lacy and Joanne come out from underneath Joanne's desk and attempt to make a run for it, but Mamba strikes at them, which forces them back beneath the desk. As the confrontation continues, Mamba begins to feel trapped and cornered. When this happens, the snake does something that brings everyone in the room to a standstill. It does what is in its nature to do, the key to its survival. It moves into striking mode. Mamba lifts around two-thirds of its body, including its head, off the floor, flattens its neck, which forms a small hood similar to that of the cobra, and delivers a loud hiss. Then the inevitable happens, Mamba displays its name-sake, its legacy, its reputation, its ultimate weapon—its mouth, the inky black mouth, which is synonymous with death, its bite 100 percent fatal without treatment. And just when it seems that Mamba has shown all it has, the snake does something absolutely chilling. It reveals its two front fangs and proceeds to secrete venom through them, which drops to the floor, as if it is self-milking, sending an intimidating message that says, "Don't fuck with me." Everyone in the room is stunned. Oh my, what a magnificent sight.

Linwood walks back into the room talking, looking down at his cell phone.

> LINWOOD
>
> I wasn't able to…

He looks up, and his cell phone drops to the floor slowly.

> LINWOOD
>
> What the hell?

With everyone distracted by Linwood's entrance into the room, Mamba takes the opportunity to flee. Everyone scrambles to get out of the building, making their way down the corridor leading to the exit door.

SCENE 20:
NEAR THE EXIT

Once they have all made their way down the corridor leading to the exit door, they soon realize their only way out has been demolished when Linwood goes to punch in the key code.

LINWOOD

What the hell happened here?

He indicates the destroyed keypad.

Lacy looks at the keypad.

LACY

Is that blood?

Jax takes a look.

> JAX

> Looks like it.

A frantic Jackie-O searches for an answer.

> JACKIE-O

> Hey, what the hell was that thing?

> CLAUDE

> I'd say a big-ass snake!

Carlos sizes things up.

> CARLOS

> It had to be fifteen to twenty feet long. And did you see that black-ass mouth? I've never seen anything like it.

Jax kneels down to the floor.

> JAX

> Hey, guys, I think this is blood over here on the floor.

Claude questions Linwood.

CLAUDE

Any luck with that keypad, man? I need to get the hell out of here.

LINWOOD

This keyboard's in bad condition. I don't think we'll be getting out this way. This keypad has taken a big hit, and on top of that, the electrical circuitry was affected when the electricity went out.

Jackie-O states the obvious.

JACKIE-O

But, Linwood, the generator kicked in. We have lights.

LINWOOD

True, but the generators Haywood bought are only big enough and strong enough to cover the lights.

JACKIE-O

Damn, figures Haywood would take the cheap way.

Jax has a bewildered look on his face.

> JAX
>
> Hang on, everyone. Something isn't
> right.

Claude looks up in the air as if to insinuate that he's tired of Jax giving orders. Lacy goes over to Jax.

> LACY
>
> What is it, Jax?

> JAX
>
> Look around. Boxes are knocked
> over; the keypad is broken; and
> there's blood. Something happened
> here, and I don't think it was any-
> thing good.

Jax slowly starts looking around, and then he stops cold. Everyone figures he's come across something, and they are right. There, lying on the floor behind the boxes, is Mr. Haywood's corpse. Lacy, startled and frightened, turns to Jax and grabs him for comfort.

> LACY
>
> Do you think that snake did this?

Claude responds in a condescending tone.

> CLAUDE
>
> Of course it did.

Carlos is very agitated at this point.

> CARLOS
>
> Look, I don't look forward to being taken out by a snake.

> CLAUDE
>
> Not me. I can't speak for the rest of you, but I'm getting the hell out of here.

Joanne, panicking and unable to gain control of her emotions, is horribly frightened.

> JOANNE
>
> I'm not going to die in here.

Lacy tries to comfort her.

> LACY
>
> Please, if we stick together, we'll be all right.

JOANNE

I'm getting out of here.

Joanne takes off running. Lacy tries to stop her.

LACY

No! Joanne, wait!

Jackie-O looks to Jax for an answer.

JACKIE-O

Man, what are we going to do? This exit is the only way out.

JAX

I don't know, but I don't intend to be its next victim.

CARLOS

Where in the hell do you think that thing came from?

JAX

I don't know, but I'd put money on the fact that it was the cause of Mason's death.

Lacy is worried about Joanne.

> LACY
>
> Jax, somebody has to go after her; she won't make it on her own with that snake out there.
>
> JAX
>
> Okay, a place as big as this one has to have more than one way out; we just have to find it. But for right now, you're right; we need to find Joanne. And, believe it or not, until we find another way out, the conference room may be the safest place.

Claude interjects arrogantly.

> CLAUDE
>
> You mean the same conference room that snake just slithered into?
>
> JAX
>
> We just need to board up and secure any openings or entrances it could get through. For now, Lacy, Jackie-O, and I will go after Joanne.

> Claude, you, Linwood, and Carlos go back to the conference room and make it as secure as possible. Everyone on board?

Claude is sarcastic.

> CLAUDE

> Okay, boss.

A few words of advice follow from Jax.

> JAX

> By the way, look around to see if you can find anything that can be used as weapons to defend yourselves just in case you come up on that snake.

> LACY

> Weapons like what?

> JAX

> Poles, sticks, metal, anything you get your hands on.

Jackie-O is being Jackie-O.

> JACKIE-O

Hell, you see that snake? Better be
a big stick.

Carlos looks at his knife with pride.

CARLOS

I don't need no stick. I got my knife.
I'll cut that bitch from head to toe
and everything in the middle.

JACKIE-O

Man, you gonna need a bigger knife
than that to bring down that snake.

SCENE 21:
SOMEWHERE IN
THE BUILDING

While everyone disburses to their designated assignments, a frantic Joanne is walking/running down hallways and corridors looking from side to side, terribly frightened, with no sense of where she is or where she's going. Jax, Lacy, and Jackie-O are cautiously looking for her in hopes of reaching her before she comes across the snake. Lacy is very worried.

>LACY
>
>Jax, we have to find her. No one
>should be alone in this building with
>that snake on the move.

Jackie-O puts his spin on things.

    JACKIE-O

    You're telling me. I've never seen
    anything like it. She shouldn't have
    taken off like that.

Jax, Lacy, and Jackie-O stop to talk.

    JAX

    Well, she's scared to death and not
    thinking straight, but this is defi-
    nitely not the time or place for her
    to be wandering off.

Lacy is ready to continue the search.

    LACY

    You're right. Let's keep moving; she
    may have gone this way.

SCENE 22:
ELSEWHERE IN THE BUILDING

Joanne, still frantic, is talking, trying to convince herself everything's going to be all right. Terrified, she hastily moves down the corridor.

JOANNE

I have to get out of here. I don't want to die here. Please, somebody get me out of here.

She's walking/running down the corridor unaware of the danger ahead. Very afraid, looking from side to side, she is determined to find a way out. Her anxiety is heightened, and so is her fear. She starts crying. Then everything seems to move in slow motion with only Joanne's back visible.

From the ceiling just above Joanne, Mamba swings down in slow motion. It strikes, retreats in normal motion, strikes again in slow motion, and retreats again in normal motion. Just then, Joanne begins to turn slowly. As a result of this action, she is now facing forward, and it becomes apparent what has just occurred. There Joanne stands, stagnated, blood running down her face, both eyeballs plucked out of their sockets. Poor Joanne stands on her feet for only a moment, and it appears she's aware of her imminent demise. She slowly drops to her knees, onto the floor, and with her last breath, she utters her final words.

JOANNE

Not me.

SCENE 23:
IN THE CORRIDOR

JAX

She probably went this way.

He indicates the hallway/corridor where poor Joanne is lying. As they reach their destination, they're astonished. Lacy grabs Jax's arm.

LACY

Oh my God!

She is horrified by Joanne's remains. Jax turns to Lacy and Jackie-O.

JAX

Come on, let's get out of here.
Nothing we can do for her now.

SCENE 24:
THE CONFERENCE ROOM

Jax, Lacy, and Jackie-O return to the conference room where they have to aggressively knock on the door to gain entrance. Claude is reluctant to open the door. He talks through the door.

CLAUDE

Who is it?

Lacy bangs on the door.

LACY

It's us. Open the door, Claude. Let us in.

CLAUDE

Are you alone?

Jackie-O is agitated.

JACKIE-O

Just open the door, man.

Claude is being an idiot as usual.

CLAUDE

How do we know, once we open the door, that snake won't come rushing in?

Linwood intervenes.

LINWOOD

Come on, Claude. Just open the door.

Claude reluctantly opens the door.

CLAUDE

I'm opening. Just make sure you don't bring any company with you.

Once Claude opens the door, Jax pushes his way through, moving Claude and grabbing him by his collar.

> JAX
>
> If you ever do that again, I'll—
>
> LINWOOD
>
> Come on, guys. We need to work together to get out of this situation.

Lacy supports Linwood.

> LACY
>
> He's right, Jax. If we plan to get out of here, we all need to work together.

Once the tempers have cooled down, Linwood asks about Joanne.

> LINWOOD
>
> Did you find Joanne?
>
> JAX
>
> Yes.

He speaks in a regretful tone.

JAX

But we were too late.

Jackie-O plays cool and fearless.

JACKIE-O

Crazy woman, if she'd just stayed calm and stayed with the rest of us...

Lacy reiterates to Jackie-O her theory on human nature.

LACY

When you're terrified, that's easier said than done.

Carlos is holding and looking at his knife.

CARLOS

Like I said, we hunt the bitch down and cut it from head to tail and everything in the middle.

Jackie-O has another reality check for Carlos.

JACKIE-O

Hell, as long as it is, reaching the tail may take a while.

CLAUDE

I'm not looking to be a hero. I just want to get the hell out of here—alive preferably.

Jax tries to be hopeful.

JAX

I'd put money on it that there's at least one other way out of here. But just in case there isn't or we're not able to find it, we need to figure out a way to survive the night. When the morning shift arrives tomorrow, they'll realize something is wrong when they can't get in. Hopefully, they'll go for help. Until then, we're on our own.

Lacy is curious.

LACY

What do you suggest we do?

Claude answers in a condescending tone.

CLAUDE

Yes, Jax, what do you suggest we do?

JAX

Look, we can't stay in this room all night just waiting for help to come. Besides, we don't know how well or for how long the barriers will hold.

LACY

What should we do?

JAX

We need to break up into groups and try to find a way out of here.

Jackie-O is not so brave now.

JACKIE-O

Man, I don't know about going out there. What if we run into that snake? It's not like we have any real weapons to defend ourselves with.

Carlos is still holding and softly rubbing his knife.

CARLOS

Speak for yourself. Like I said, as long as I have old Mojoe with me, I will be getting out of here.

JACKIE-O

And like I said before, you'd better have something bigger than that if you intend to go up against what's out there and live to talk about it.

Linwood offers some encouragement.

LINWOOD

Look, I have a little experience in electrical work. I used to tag along with my father, who was the neighborhood handyman—one of his many trades. Working on electrical boxes and switches was something he did a lot of. I think I remember some of that stuff. I'll go back to the exit area and try to fix the electrical box. While I'm at it, I'll try to rewire that keypad since it seems to be the only way out. Anyone want to team up with me?

Jackie-O, looking away, notices that no one is volunteering.

> JACKIE-O
>
> I'll go with you.
>
> JAX
>
> Lacy and I will take the west end. This is a large facility. Maybe the occupants who were here before left something we can use against this monster.

Claude looks over at Carlos.

> CLAUDE
>
> I guess that just leaves you and me.

Carlos answers in a nonchalant tone.

> CARLOS
>
> I guess so.
>
> CLAUDE
>
> May as well start at the opposite end.

Jax gives a word of advice.

JAX

Everyone, keep your eyes open, stay alert, and if you come across any-thing better than what you already have to use as a weapon, grab it.

Responses are slow. They all nod in agreement.

JAX

Okay, we'll meet back here in, say, an hour.

Again, everyone disburses to their designated location.

SCENE 25:
THE WEST END OF
THE BUILDING

As Jax and Lacy are cautiously looking for a way out, or anything that may help them survive the night, Jax comes up with a suggestion.

> JAX
>
> While we're looking for a way out, maybe we can find something that will give us an idea as to where or how this snake came to be.
>
> LACY
>
> Jax, I just want to say that no matter how this turns out, I'm happy to be

in this predicament with someone like you.

Jax is modest.

JAX

Don't make me a hero yet, especially since—

He stops and does not continue his thought. She encourages him to continue.

LACY

Go ahead. What is it?

JAX

It's nothing. I just don't like for people to expect too much, get too close.

Lacy shares an observation of him.

LACY

I must admit, ever since we met, I've felt there's something you're holding inside, something heavy. I know this sounds strange, considering we've just met and I don't know

anything about you, but that's what
I've sensed.

Jax is in a solemn mood.

> JAX
>
> Sometimes things happen in life you
> wish you could forget, but the con-
> science just won't let you.

She senses he has a painful secret, so she lets up.

> LACY
>
> Okay, but if you ever feel like vent-
> ing, I'm a good listener.

> JAX
>
> I'll remember that. But for now, our
> time and energy is needed to find a
> way out of here.

So they proceed on their way looking for a way out.

SCENE 26:
THE EXIT DOOR

Over at the entrance/exit area of the facility, Linwood is working on the electrical box with Jackie-O assisting him. Jackie-O shares his thoughts.

> JACKIE-O
>
> Man, I sure hope you know what you're doing. This whole thing is absolutely crazy. It's like being in a movie.
>
> LINWOOD
>
> Believe me, I want out of here as bad as you do.

Linwood pauses for a moment.

> LINWOOD

> By the way, in this movie, unlike the real movies, once you're dead, you're dead.

> JACKIE-O

> Thanks, I feel a whole lot worse.

Linwood just smiles.

SCENE 27:
THE EAST END OF
THE BUILDING

Over on the east end of the building, Claude and Carlos are searching for a way out. Carlos is enthused by what he sees.

CARLOS

Man, look, a fitness room.

He proceeds toward the room. Claude grabs Carlos by the arm.

CLAUDE

Hey, Hercules, where are you going?

Carlos pulls his arm away from Claude.

> CARLOS
>
> Look, I can't just pass a gym and not go in.
>
> CLAUDE
>
> Are you crazy? There's a hundred-foot snake out there waiting to do us in, and you're looking to get in a workout? You're crazy.

Carlos is playing the big man.

> CARLOS
>
> Man, I ain't scared of no damn snake.

Claude tries to convince him that they need to move on.

> CLAUDE
>
> Look, we need to find a way out of here or at least something we can use as real weapons to protect ourselves.

Carlos is holding and rotating his knife as if examining it.

CARLOS

I told you all I need is this right here.

Then he starts to swing it about as if in hand-to-hand combat.

CLAUDE

Okay, do what you have to do, but
I'm going to keep moving.

CARLOS

Go on, I'll catch up to you.

Claude looks at Carlos, shrugs his shoulders, and walks off.

Carlos is talking to himself.

CARLOS

Bitch, better not fuck with me. I'm
a Rican.

Then he notices a piece of exercise equipment.

CARLOS

Oh snap, one of those exercise
machines with the rods!

He proceeds toward the machine to inspect it. He places his knife on a chair, reaches for a towel lying on the back of the chair, and wraps it around his neck.

CARLOS

Hell, it's an old one, but it'll do.

Then Carlos notices a bench press in front of the machine facing a wall of full-length mirrors. He sits on the bench with his legs straddling it. Facing the mirrors, he turns and reaches over his right shoulder to attach the power rods to the cable for his desired resistance and does the same for his left side. Once the connections are complete, Carlos grabs the handgrips and begins his workout, huffing and puffing, inhaling, exhaling, and giving it all he's got.

CARLOS

That bitch thinks she can mess with
me. She don't know I'm a Rican.

He performs several reps, and then he's tired, so he takes a short break. He starts again, working as hard as he can, pushing it to the max, alternating between pectoral, triceps, abdominal, and deltoid muscle groups. He admires himself in a mirror directly in front of him as he moves through a series of positions exhibiting his masculine physique saturated in sweat. Once he finishes his reps, he uses the towel wrapped around his neck to wipe the sweat from

his head, brow, neck, face, and eyes. As he's wiping his
eyes, which are not yet in focus, he thinks he sees something move behind him in the mirrors, but there couldn't
be, because the only thing behind him is the extra power
rods. He's blinking, his eyes still trying to get into focus.
As he continues to sit on the exercise bench facing the
wall of mirrors, he has no doubt something's behind him.
He's becoming uneasy, anxious, his eyes locked in on the
mirrors in front of him. He continues to sit on the bench.
Then it happens. Mamba slowly starts to separate itself
from the power rods it has so cleverly camouflaged itself
within. Carlos looks on in amazement, paralyzed, frozen.
He's afraid to move, cough, or even breathe, a hostage on
an exercise bench. Then it comes to him, *His knife!* But it's
on the chair about a foot away. Carlos sits on the exercise
bench, anticipating his move for the knife, but he's seen
Mamba in action. He knows going for it would be a fifty-
fifty chance, but he has to take it—and he does.

SCENE 28:
ELSEWHERE IN THE BUILDING

As Jax and Lacy continue to search for another way out, Jax wanders upon a seam on the wall, which appears to be a sealed door.

> JAX
>
> There appears to be some type of seam here.

He puts his hands there and attempts to pull at it.

> JAX
>
> I need something to wedge through here. Hey, hand me that metal bar over there in the corner.

Lacy goes over, picks up the bar, and hands it to Jax, who uses it to try to pry the door open. The door pops open.

> JAX
>
> Got it.

As he wedges the bar in the seam, Jax slowly pushes the door open. The room looks as if it is some type of laboratory or medical facility; Jax and Lacy proceed into the room…cautiously.

> JAX
>
> From the look of things, some-one was conducting some type of research or something in here.
>
> LACY
>
> Well, whoever was here must have had to leave in a hurry, because they left a lot of stuff behind.
>
> JAX
>
> Take a look around. See if you can find anything we may be able to use as weapons…and Lacy…

She turns to him.

JAX

Be careful.

The two proceed with their search, looking around, opening closet doors, flipping through papers, etc.

LACY

Jackpot.

Jax goes over to see what Lacy has found.

LACY

Someone felt they needed some heavy artillery.

Jax picks up a few of the weapons, calling them by name.

JAX

I agree. M16s, M4 carbines, M240 machine guns, hand grenades, you name it; they have it. A lot of this stuff would be used by special ops.

Lacy's impressed.

LACY

You really know your weapons.

Jax responds in a low tone.

> JAX
>
> You can say that. Hey, grab every-
> thing you can.

Jax grabs a bag.

> JAX
>
> Here, put as many as you can in
> here.

He notices some bullets.

> JAX
>
> Put these in, too. Now let's see if we
> can find anything that can help us
> with our adversary.

Jax starts shuffling through some papers on a desk.

> JAX
>
> Hey, come over here. I think I may
> have found something.

Lacy approaches him.

> LACY
>
> What is this stuff?

Jax looks at what appears to be sketches.

> JAX
>
> It looks like some type of diagram or something.
>
> LACY
>
> It looks like a snake.
>
> JAX
>
> Look here.

Jax points to one of the diagrams.

> JAX
>
> Does this look like the snake that came after us?
>
> LACY
>
> Yes, but just smaller.

Jax flips through more papers.

> JAX
>
> Listen to this: "the black mamba"—at least we have a name now—"as it is called, is the longest, fastest, and deadliest venomous snake on land."

Lacy responds in an unsettled tone.

> LACY
>
> Sounds like we may be in major trouble.
>
> JAX
>
> Look over here.

He indicates what appears to be information related to genetic engineering.

> JAX
>
> It would seem whoever was here was working on expanding this snake's skills. The people who were working on this project obviously knew the chances they were taking and felt the need to be fully armed in case their "prodigy" got out of control.

Jax gathers the papers.

> JAX
>
> Look, we can try and make sense out of some of this stuff when we get back to the conference room.

Lacy questions him in a concerned tone.

> LACY
>
> Jax, are we going to make it out of here alive?
>
> JAX
>
> I don't know, but one thing is for sure: we can't allow that snake out into the general population.

Lacy gestures in agreement.

> LACY
>
> Come on, let's go.

Jax and Lacy pick up the bags filled with ammunition to carry back to the conference room, but before they leave, Jax turns back and grabs all the paperwork and diagrams related to the mamba from the desk. Then he notices a microcassette player, which he also picks up.

> JAX
>
> I want to learn as much as possible about our adversary, and this cassette may have something on it that could help us.

Jax and Lacy cautiously leave the lab en route back to the conference room to meet up with the rest of the group. On their way back, they come across the gym where Carlos was last seen. He is still there, a sight to be seen, stretched out on the bench press, dead of course. There is nothing they can do, so they leave him there.

SCENE 29:
BACK IN
THE CONFERENCE ROOM

Everyone meets back in the conference room as sched-
uled. Jax unloads the bag of weapons.

JACKIE-O

Oh snap!

He is ogling to the assortment of weapons Jax and Lacy
had returned with.

JACKIE-O

You guys hit the megaload!

JAX

We found it in a concealed room over on the west end of the building.

Linwood walks over and starts talking to Jax.

LINWOOD

Did you see Claude and Carlos?

Jax shakes his head and answers under his breath.

JAX

Carlos didn't make it. Didn't see Claude. How is the electrical box coming along?

LINWOOD

I'll need more time.

JAX

More time is something we don't have.

Claude enters the conference room, and Jackie-O goes over to him.

JACKIE-O

Check out the ammo Jax and Lacy found.

Claude responds condescendingly.

CLAUDE

Jax to the rescue again.

JACKIE-O

Hey, where's Carlos?

CLAUDE

I don't know.

Jackie-O is bewildered.

JACKIE-O

You don't know? What do you mean you don't know?

CLAUDE

Like I said, I don't know. We were looking for a way out; he saw a gym and said he was going to get a workout.

Lacy is angry.

LACY

So you just left him there without a thought or care of what could happen to him?

Claude answers her in his usual uncaring tone.

CLAUDE

Look, we went off together as a team looking for a way out; I'm not his babysitter.

JAX

Carlos didn't make it. He was still in the gym where you left him. But for now, we need to learn as much as possible about this snake. Take a look at what else we found in that concealed room.

Jax spreads the diagrams and papers he found out on the table. Linwood takes a look.

LINWOOD

What's that?

JAX

Hopefully, our key to survival until we find a way out of here.

Jax proceeds to read from the documents.

JAX

It says here this snake is called the "black mamba," scientific name *Dendro-aspis po-ly-lepis.*

He pronounces the scientific name, but with some difficulty.

JAX

"The black mamba lives in South Africa in such habitats as the savannas, open woodlands, and rocky places, and is considered one of the most deadly venomous snakes in the world—"

JACKIE-O

Well, how did it get here?

Jax continues to read.

JAX

"They are also considered the fastest snake on land, reaching speeds of ten to twelve miles per hour, and the longest venomous snake, some reaching lengths of fourteen feet."

Claude throws in his two cents.

CLAUDE

Fourteen feet, my ass, that snake has to be at least twenty feet if not more.

JAX

"When striking, the black mamba is able to lift two-thirds of its body off the ground and can strike from a distance of four to six feet away."

The faces in the room have expressions of doom.

JAX

"The name 'black mamba' is not attributed to the body color of this snake, which can be various shades of gray, but to the inky black inside of its mouth. This snake is amongst the most venomous snakes in the world. The black mamba's fangs are located in the rear of its mouth and are able to hold up to twenty drops of venom. A single bite from this snake has enough venom to kill twenty to forty grown men."

Jackie-O is feeling hopeless.

JACKIE-O

Man, we'll never get out of here alive.

Jax continues to share the gloomy facts.

JAX

"Death from this snake's bite is 100 percent certain without treatment." But, guys, there's something here that's optimistic.

Lacy is hopeful.

LACY

What's that?

JAX

It says here that black mambas are very nervous snakes and tend to avoid contact with humans.

Jackie-O states the obvious.

JACKIE-O

Hell, this one sure isn't shy. It went out of its way to make sure we knew it was here. It attacked us.

JAX

That's because this one is not the norm.

Claude is curious.

CLAUDE

What do you mean?

JAX

Take a look at these diagrams and equations.

Jax spreads out the papers with the genetic acceleration/enhancement information.

JAX

I'm no biology major, but I'd put money on it that someone has been tampering with Mother Nature.

Jackie-O jumps in.

JACKIE-O

You mean some kind of mad scientist built this snake?

Claude criticizes the group.

CLAUDE

You guys are a bunch of idiots. You've been watching too much bullshit on television.

Lacy breaks in.

LACY

After what we've seen and now this, maybe it is possible.

LINWOOD

If all this is true, it would explain the need for the heavy artillery.

Jax pulls out a microcassette player.

> JAX
>
> I picked this up on the way out of the room.
>
> JACKIE-O
>
> What is it?
>
> JAX
>
> A microcassette player. I grabbed it, hoping it might have something on it we can use.

Linwood is excited.

> LINWOOD
>
> Okay, let's check it out.

Jax pushes the "play" button on the microcassette player, and the dialogue begins.

> DR. STANFORD
>
> Dr. Neal Stanford, lead genetic engineer. There are those who would refer to me as insane, a mad scientist, but I assure you, mad I am not.

I am about to embark on a quest in the world of genetic engineering never before attempted—genetically engineered black mambas created by man not by God. I, Dr. Neal Stanford, am creator and controller of what will soon be man's most notorious and dangerous adversary. Dictators will search me out; world leaders will offer me their souls; and those who ridiculed me will bow before me. There are those who will oppose me, question my sanity and consider my actions a vendetta against humanity. Perhaps they are correct for it is humanity who ridiculed and ostracized my work and for this it is humanity who will pay the price---that I promise. Here we have two black mambas, a male and a female; they will be my first test subjects.

December 17, 9:00 a.m.—The first series of genetically altered hormones has been injected in a male and female black mamba; no adverse side effects have been noted.

January 15, 9:15 a.m.—The second series of hormones has been injected into the mambas. They appear to be tolerating the injections; no complications noted.

February 16, 9:20 a.m.—The final series of injections have been administered.

April 17—Female mamba has successfully copulated while in captivity following a series of injections of genetically altered hormones.

June 20—Female mamba lays four genetically engineered/enhanced eggs.

September 22—All four eggs have hatched.

October 1—It's only been ten days since the hatching and the snakes are growing at a rapid rate, aggression escalating.

October 28—Two techs and three armed guards have been killed by the mambas. The snakes are out of control. Cannot handle, cannot take a chance on my work being discovered; will have to be destroyed.

October 30—All four snakes have been contained and destroyed, but make no mistake: my work is not over. It will never end, not until I create the ultimate weapon, the ultimate creation.

Jax turns the microcassette player off.

LINWOOD

Yes, this would explain the need for the heavy artillery. But according to Stanford, all the snakes were destroyed.

JAX

Obviously, there's still one. Maybe one got away, and they missed it. Something happened.

Jackie-O is nervous.

JACKIE-O

If all this is true, we can't afford to stick around here waiting to be rescued. We need to find a way out of here—now.

LINWOOD

I agree.

Linwood looks to Jax.

LINWOOD

What's the plan?

JAX

Linwood, you and Jackie-O get back to work on that electrical box. Lacy and I will continue looking for a way out. There were several other corridors and hallways we didn't get a chance to check out.

He turns to Claude.

JAX

Carlos didn't make it, but you're welcome to join Lacy and me.

CLAUDE

No, thanks, chief. I think I'll go it alone; unlike the others, I don't need your protection. I'm more than able to take care of myself.

JAX

Suit yourself.

Jax starts issuing the weapons.

JAX

We have an M16. It's lightweight and simple to operate.

He turns to Lacy.

JAX

Have any experience with guns?

LACY

I hung out with a guy who was really into guns; he taught me a thing or two. I learned a little from him on how to handle them.

JAX

Think you can handle it?

She looks it over.

LACY

They weren't M16s, but I think I can handle this.

JAX

Okay we have a couple of semiautomatics and an M240 machine gun.

Jackie-O jumps up.

JACKIE-O

I'll take that.

He points to the M240.

JACKIE-O

I always wanted to get my hands on one of these.

JAX

That's a good choice. It's a reliable weapon and bumps a lot of rounds. Just be careful.

Claude walks over and picks out his own weapon.

CLAUDE

I'll be taking this one.

He picks up the M4 carbine.

CLAUDE

This baby is used by special ops; this is right up my alley.

Jax gives a warning.

JAX

Heads up, everyone; we've seen what this snake can do, and according to what we now know, it's nothing to mess with. But most important, remember that the role of predator versus prey has made an unfortunate turnaround. It's anybody's guess as to whether or not we're all going to make it out of here. So good luck. Stay alert, and stay alive.

Everyone disburses to their designated locations.

SCENE 30:
SOMEWHERE IN THE
UNDERGROUND WAREHOUSE

Jax and Lacy cautiously case the different areas of this large underground warehouse. With the uncertainty of their future, Lacy appeals to Jax to unburden himself of whatever's haunting him.

LACY

I know this is not the time for soul-baring but if we're going to die together, it would be nice to know a little about who I died with.

JAX

There's not much.

Lacy responds in a cheerful manner.

> LACY
>
> No, no, no, don't do that.
>
> JAX
>
> Do what?
>
> LACY
>
> You know what. Pretend that you're an uninteresting, regular Joe. From the first time I saw you, I knew better than that.
>
> JAX
>
> Pretty big assumption about someone you don't even know.
>
> LACY
>
> Well, you don't have to know a person to know they either have something to hide or something's haunting them.

He tries to derail her interest.

JAX

For someone being stalked by a killer snake, you sure are pretty chatty.

She tries to use mild humor to relax him.

LACY

Well, faced with death, venting seems to be the only thing that's helping me keep my sanity; besides, whatever is shared in lieu of death follows in death.

She moves to serious mode and comes in closer to him, mildly comforting him.

LACY

Talk to me. Whatever it is, I'm not going to judge you. You can trust me. I just want to help.

Jax is about to share with Lacy, but he pauses.

Lacy assures him in a serious tone.

LACY

It's okay, Jax. You can talk to me.

JAX

Talk to you? I don't even think I've
ever been able to say the words out
loud. But they seem to speak loud
and clear in my head every minute
of every day.

He appears to be unable to finish his story. She comforts
him.

LACY

Please talk to me.

He pauses.

JAX

I killed a child.

He sinks into sorrow.

He separates himself from her and walks away as he tells
his story—a deep, dark story, the kind of story that epito-
mizes that adage that it only takes a split second to ruin
the rest of your life and someone else's.

JAX

About twenty years ago, I had just
returned home from the Gulf War.

LACY

You were in Desert Storm?

She pauses.

LACY

That's how you knew about all those weapons.

JAX

He flashes back as he tells his story.

Yes…Anyway I had seen things over there, did things, endured the loss of men I'd come to consider friends. I knew when I left, I had some issues, unresolved issues— anger being one of them—but I figured once I was back in the States, things would work themselves out. But they didn't. Help was available for me, but I didn't seek it, so I continued to spiral downhill. It wasn't obvious in my everyday life, but it was something on the inside, something others couldn't see, but I felt. So about fifteen years ago, I had been working at the local shipyard. It was a going-nowhere-fast job, but I needed something; bills needed to be paid. Anyway, one evening on my way home from work, another car cut me off, jumped right out in front of me, no signal or nothing. Well, I cursed, flipped the finger, blew the horn, you name it, but I couldn't just let it go at that. I took off after this car, and once I caught up to it, without really looking, I jumped in the lane behind it not realizing that another car was merging into that lane.

He pauses.

JAX

So my car and the other car ended up sideswiping each other, causing that car to lose control.

He works hard to hold his composure.

JAX

My actions caused that car to run off the road and into a ravine.

He stares into space as he proceeds with his story.

JAX

In the back of that car was a car seat with a three-year-old in it, wearing a little private school uniform. Anyway, the impact was so severe that the child suffered internal injuries, and he died on the way to the hospital. There were witnesses at the scene who reported that I was driving erratically and caused the accident. I was later brought up on charges of involuntary manslaughter. I didn't contest it. I had no defense for my behavior, and I knew whatever the judge handed down, I deserved. But the attorney I had knew my history, so he used that information during my trial for leniency. At my sentencing, the judge took everything into consideration and sentenced me to one year of jail time, community service when released, and mandatory mental health services, preferably through the VA.

Pause.

JAX

Well that's my story. Still think I'm some sort of hero?

She looks on from a distance with sadness in her eyes.

LACY

I think you're a man with a past who can't find peace.

JAX

Peace—actually not having any is my true punishment.

LACY

You made a mistake, a horrible mistake. I know something about making mistakes, and they all started for me at an early age—I think that's what drew me to you. As a young girl I was what they call today permissive. All the girls my age hated me and I would pretend it didn't bother me----but it did. But as an adult I came to the reality that those mistakes did not have to define me.

Jax cuts Lacy off.

JAX

Look, I made a mistake that cost a life, a child's life. There's no coming back from that, so please don't try and comfort me. There's nothing you or anyone can say that will take this all away.

Lacy replies in a calm tone.

LACY

I'm not trying to tell you how to feel or even trying to convince you that what you're feeling is wrong, because anyone with a conscience and a soul would feel exactly as you do after hurting a child. But what I am trying to say to you is give yourself a second chance, Jax. What happened is tragic and will always be with you, but you deserve to get out of here. Jax, you deserve to live… Okay?"

He lightens up a little.

> JAX
>
> From your mouth to God's ears.
>
> LACY
>
> Okay, so come on; let's find a way
> out of this hell.

Jax nods his head in agreement, and the two proceed with their search.

SCENE 31:
THE FUSE BOX

Down the corridor, where the fuse box is located, Linwood and Jackie-O are working on restoring the electricity. Jackie-O is talking continuously as usual.

JACKIE-O

Look, I'm not trying to rush you or anything, but how much longer until this electricity is back up and running?

Linwood continues diligently working.

LINWOOD

As you know, I'm no licensed elec-
trician. I don't even know if what
I'm doing will work, but to do nothing is certain death.

Jackie-O lifts his head and stops talking, as if he hears
something.

JACKIE-O

Hey, did you hear that?

LINWOOD

Hear what? I didn't hear anything.

Jackie-O is convinced he heard something.

JACKIE-O

Well, I did.

He points across the room.

JACKIE-O

Right over there.

LINWOOD

Well, go and check it out.

JACKIE-O

Check it out? Are you crazy? It could
be that snake.

Linwood displays his happy-go-lucky disposition.

LINWOOD

Or it could be a mouse. Go check
it out. I think I'm almost finished
here.

JACKIE-O

Shoot, you crazy man. I'm a player,
not some kind of Indiana Jones.
What you trying to do? Use me as
snake bait?

Linwood smiles as he continues to work.

LINWOOD

Go ahead. I have your back.
Anyways, that snake is not shy. If it
were over there, we'd know it.

Jackie-O proceeds with the search cautiously.

JACKIE-O

Hey, man, I think you're right. All I
see over here is some rat poof. Sure
need to clean this place up. By the
way, for the record, I wasn't scared
to come over here.

There's silence from Linwood, but Jackie-O continues to
talk. Jackie-O turns to Linwood.

JACKIE-O

Hey, look.

As Jackie-O turns toward Linwood, he notices he's just
standing there expressionless, powerless, and motionless,
with the exception of some mild shaking and tremors.
There is foam coming from his mouth, which descends to
his chin before dropping onto the floor. Jackie-O stands
there paralyzed with fear as this drama unfolds, terrified
as to how it's going to end. Then poor Linwood drops
to the floor, and who's directly behind him? Mamba—
mouth wide open, fangs positioned, a black hole of death.
Jackie-O stands there trembling with fear, only allowing
his eyes to travel from side to side looking for the gun. But
unlike Carlos, Jackie-O is no hero, so he opts to run. And
run he does, with Mamba right on his trail.

SCENE 32:
SOMEWHERE IN
THE UNDERGROUND
WAREHOUSE/POSSIBLE EXIT

Jax and Lacy continue examining the walls, looking for any sign of a way out or an area that can be removed in order to gain entrance to the outside.

Jax turns to Lacy.

JAX

Did you feel that?

LACY

Feel what?

JAX

Feels like a breeze coming from somewhere.

He continues examining the wall.

JAX

Usually, where there's a breeze, there's an opening. Come on, keep looking.

He locates the source of the breeze and starts pulling at the wall.

JAX

I think I found something over here.

Lacy runs over to help Jax pull away at the structure, but the two are not enough.

JAX

We'll need more manpower. Let's get the others.

SCENE 33:
IN ANOTHER PART OF
THE WAREHOUSE

Claude, now in renegade mood, is cautiously casing the ceilings and corridors, hunting what he now considers a trophy for the highest bidder.

Claude talks to himself.

> CLAUDE
>
> Mamba, Mamba, where are you, Mamba? I'm sure there's a bounty on your head. Dead or alive, a snake like you should be worth something.

Jax and Lacy stumble upon Claude, startling him, and he reacts by swinging his gun around and pointing it at them.

JAX

Hold on, it's just us. I think we may
have found a way out of here. Air
was coming through the walls over
there.

He points in the direction they'd just come from.

CLAUDE

Hey, did you hear that?

Jax turns and looks in the direction Claude's looking.

JAX

Hear what?

CLAUDE

Your executioner.

At the far end of hall is Mamba making its way toward
them, Claude turns and goes into the room directly
behind him, locking the door, preventing Jax and Lacy
from entering. Jax and Lacy bang at the door, insisting
that Claude open it but soon realize he's not letting them
in. They take off running, cursing Claude.

JAX

I'll get you for this, Cooper!

Claude is laughing hysterically, talking to himself.

> CLAUDE
>
> Let's see how much of a hero he is
> now.

Claude gains his composure in what he considers his sanctuary and decides to have a smoke. So he flops down in a chair and takes a cigarette out of his chest pocket.

> CLAUDE
>
> I haven't had one of these in weeks,
> but I deserve it.

He starts searching about his person, looking for his lighter, which he eventually finds in his back pants pocket. But as he's attempting to flick the lighter, it drops onto the floor. Claude bends down, retrieves it, sits back in the chair, lights the cigarette, and proceeds to smoke. He is becoming very relaxed. His eyes are heavy; it appears he may even fall asleep. His eyes are becoming heavier, so he closes them; he opens them, and he closes them again. But this time, he leaves them closed for a second or so. When he opens them this time, while drawing a puff of his cigarette, he discovers Mamba is right in front of him. It lunges forward and strikes Claude directly in the forehead with its venomous fangs. Since the venom has not yet taken full effect, Claude jumps to his feet, grabs hold of Mamba, whose fangs are still attached to his fore-head. Claude holds onto Mamba. The two thrash about as if dancing. Mamba, being true to its nature, maintains its hold until Claude succumbs to the venom and drops to the floor, his dying body still thrashing slightly, with the lit cigarette between his severely swollen and pinched lips. His last breath was a last puff.

SCENE 34:
BACK AT THE POSSIBLE EXIT

Jax and Lacy rush back to the location where they felt the breeze of air.

Jax pulls away at the wood and debris blocking the area where the breeze is coming from.

> JAX
>
> Come on, give me a hand.

Jax and Lacy work diligently to remove the obstacles in the way of their freedom, but they do not work fast enough, because Mamba is soon upon them. Mamba attempts to strike at Jax and Lacy, but they defend themselves with the weapons they acquired from the lab. A direct hit seems impossible, given Mamba's speed and agility. Jax and Lacy continue to try to ward off Mamba, but the snake is too fast, so retreating seems the most feasible thing to do. But Mamba corners them near the area of the breeze. The rest of the debris comes down on Jax and Lacy, trapping them underneath. Meanwhile, Mamba makes its great escape through a hole in the wall. It has gained access to the world outside the facility, the one place they did not want it to be.

It is daybreak the next morning. At this point, Mamba has gone beyond the confines of the facility into what appears to be an industrialized area, an area that is being underused with not much activity and where the homeless might migrate. Mamba has exited the building and is en route to the general public when it stumbles upon an elderly vagrant, staggering along, singing to himself. He stops to take a gulp from his liquor bottle, a cheap bottle of wine, to be precise. As the vagrant's head is tilted backward, so tilted it looks as if it could roll off, and the bottom of his wine bottle is up in the air, he's able to see through the glass an image, an image rising up into the sky. Now he starts to lower his bottle slowly. With the bottle down, he sees Mamba towering above him, a good fourteen feet taller than himself. He swallows his drink, which you could hear a mile away, and then he scrunches his eyes in amazement at what's in front of him. There Mamba stands, moving slowly and gracefully as if floating. It is an image of pure arrogance. Mamba has an air of superiority, glaring down on the vagrant, who looks like a speck in comparison. The vagrant stands there looking up at what appears to be a giant, a god. Mamba exhales a hiss. It is like nothing the vagrant has ever heard before, a hiss so intimidating he wets his pants.

By now, Jax and Lacy have worked their way from beneath the debris and come running outside the building after Mamba. Jax starts shooting at the snake, which forces Mamba back into the building, and the vagrant takes off running. Jax and Lacy follow Mamba back into the building, at which time there is a stand-off between man and snake. Lacy has a gun. She's trying to shoot Mamba, but because of the snake's speed and her lack of experience with firearms, her attempts are futile. With its tail, it knocks her across the room, rendering her unconscious.

Now Jax and Mamba come to a face-off. At first, Jax tries to hit Mamba with a bullet, but the snake knocks the weapon from his hand. Jax comes face-to-face with Mamba. The snake is moving in closer and closer to Jax, invading all his space, until Jax's back is up against a pole, at which time, Mamba proceeds in fast motion rapidly wrapping itself around the pole and Jax from the bottom up. It pins Jax to the pole, until it reaches Jax's face. Its coils are covering his mouth, leaving only his forehead, eyes, and chin visible. There Mamba hovers in front of Jax. They are eye to eye. Just as it becomes apparent that

Mamba has become weary of its opponent and is about to strike, the snake becomes motionless and starts to drop to the floor in what appears to be pieces. Now free, Jax runs over to check on Lacy, and she starts to come around.

Lacy is a little disoriented.

> LACY
>
> What happened?
>
> JAX
>
> It's all over now. You're all right.

Lacy takes in the condition of Mamba.

> LACY
>
> How did you do it?

Jax holds up Carlos's hunting knife.

> JAX
>
> I doubled back and grabbed it from the exercise room; figured poor Carlos didn't need it any longer.

Lacy, still on the floor, wraps her arms around Jax, expressing her relief and appreciation to him for saving them. Just when it looks as if it's all over, a noise comes from the other side of the room. Automatically, Jax and Lacy jump into defensive mode in response to the noise they've just heard. Jax gestures to Lacy to stay on the floor; he slowly retrieves one of the automatic weapons and proceeds in the direction of the noise. As Jax gets closer, the noise gets louder, so much louder that Jax is about to spray the area with bullets. But at the last moment, the source of the noise is revealed. It is Jackie-O; he made it.

> JAX
>
> Man, I thought you'd been taken out.

Jackie-O plays macho.

> JACKIE-O
>
> Are you kidding? Man, ain't no snake gonna take out a player.

> JAX
>
> Anyway, I'm just glad you're still with us.

They go to help Lacy to her feet. Jax is relieved to be alive.

> JAX
>
> Let's get out of here.

Lacy jokes.

LACY

I think I'll call in sick today.

The three proceed to walk away.

THE END

EPILOGUE

In a desolate location are Dr. Stanford and his faithful companion Dr. Merit up to their old tricks.

Dr. Merit walks over to Dr. Stanford who is standing in front of a glass incubator.

>   DR. MERIT
>
>   How long doctor until your genius
>   is revealed?

Dr. Stanford stands there quiet, preoccupied, gazing through the glass.

>   DR. STANFORD
>
>   Soon doctor, very soon.

Inside the incubator is about a half dozen abnormally large, misshapen eggs, bulging, eager to get out....then one splits.

ABOUT THE AUTHOR

Angela Dungee-Farley is the wife of Dennis Farley and the mother of Daniel Farley, currently residing in New York. Dungee-Farleys' passion for horror began at a very early age eight or nine years old to be exact. She remembers as a young girl not attending the local high school athletic events, if it meant missing any of her weekly horror shows.

As an adult her passion for horror grew with her, so one day she decided to write a horror herself........and so she did. Mamba is Dungee-Farley's first published book.

ABOUT THE BOOK

Dr. Neal Stanford, A brilliant Scientist, specializing in the field of Genetic Engineering, harboring a vendetta against humanity for its scrutiny and criticism of his vision. Those who worked alongside the doctor, questioned and feared his moral and ethical values. They soon realized his ideas, if allowed to manifest would be detrimental. And for nine unsuspecting people trapped in an abandoned underground facility, Dr. Stanfords' vision was all too real. Dr. Stanford had genetically engineered black mamba snakes. This snake in its own rights was already perfection, feared by all who crossed its path, and inferior to no other creature than man. The latter, a fact Dr. Stanford was determined to change. His goal was to create mambas "God" did not have a hand in, Mambas that would not scurry when man approach and mambas that do not simply hunt to survive. But instead mambas that would be the hunters of man.....and so he did. So come along, slither with me through a night of fright, dismay and death, lets see who if any will make it out alive against the new superior creature......Mamba.

30778610R00108

Made in the USA
Charleston, SC
26 June 2014